First published 2021 by Lusiana Austin

Copyright © Lusiana Austin 2021

A CIP record for this book is available at the National Library of Australia.

ISBN 978-0-6453063-0-9
eBook 978-0-6453063-1-6

Jack's Visit to Cowra

By Lusi Austin

ACKNOWLEDGEMENTS

I acknowledge the custodians of this land, the Wiradjuri people, on whose land this story was written and pay my respects to their elders past, present and emerging.

I also acknowledge the incredible efforts of so many who have gone before us to keep safe the stories of The Breakout for future generations.

I give special acknowledgement to Lawrance Ryan, Graham Apthorpe and the entire Cowra Breakout Association without whose support this book would not have been possible.

Thank you to Stassi Austin for your help editing this book and being my sounding board.

Enormous gratitude to Kim Kelly for kindly assisting me in the book's final stages.

And to every person who takes the time to read this book and keep the story of hope and peace alive...

Thank you.
Lusi x

DEDICATION

For all those who lost their lives in The Breakout and for those who have dedicated their lives since to the path of peace.

To Cowra for adopting us as family.

For my parents who gave me a love of literature and history.

For my husband Brett, my children Stassi, Elijah, Ethan, Zipporah and Ezekiel – I love you all endlessly.

Coming home from school on a Friday
is the best feeling ever.

I dump my bag on the kitchen bench and forget all about school.

"The weekend is finally here!"

I especially love the weekends when I get to go with Dad
to visit Gran and Pa's farm out in Cowra.

We pack a bag of clothes and
special snacks for the drive out there.

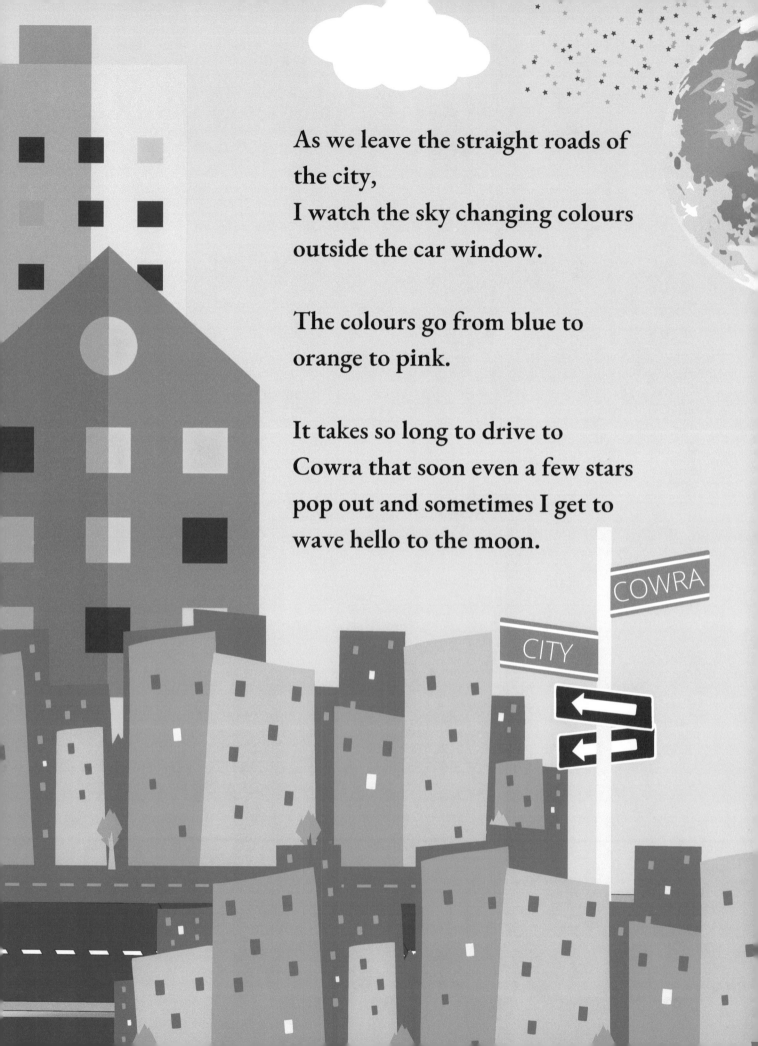

As we leave the straight roads of the city,
I watch the sky changing colours outside the car window.

The colours go from blue to orange to pink.

It takes so long to drive to Cowra that soon even a few stars pop out and sometimes I get to wave hello to the moon.

We travel over the mountains.

Sometimes we stop to fill up the car with petrol and Dad lets me choose a chocolate bar at the counter of the shop.

I ask Dad, "How far is it to Cowra now?" Dad says, "Not too far. I've got to be careful I don't hit any roos."

I don't remember getting to Gran and Pa's place this time. I think I fell asleep in the car.

Dad must have carried me inside their house because the next morning, I hear a loud rooster calling and it wakes me up!

I run outside and call to Gran and Pa.

"There's our little city slicker," Gran says as I run to give them a big cuddle.

Gran smells like apples and the pies she sometimes bakes. Pa roughs up my hair and says, "G'day little mate!"

I help Pa feed the chickens.

"Watch that rooster," he reminds me. "He gets a bit cranky sometimes. He's a bit like the rooster I had as a kid," says Pa.

"What was it like when you were a kid Pa?" I ask.

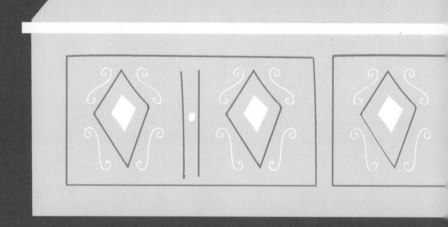

"Times were tough back then," Pa replies.
"After school, I did farm chores. It was my
job to feed the chickens every day.

"Want to know the strangest thing I ever
saw in our chook house?" Pa asks me.

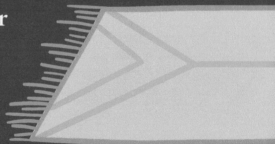

"What Pa?"

"A Japanese man!"

"Why was there a Japanese man in your chook house? How did he get there?" I say.

"Well, back in that time, there was a big war going on in the world. It was called the Second World War. Australia and some other countries were on one side and Japan and another lot of countries were on the other side," explains Pa.

"But how did that man get all the way from Japan into your chook house, Pa?" I question.

"You know how Cowra is far away from the ocean? Well it was chosen as a place to bring lots of Japanese men who'd been captured during the war. If they tried to leave Cowra, it would be a long walk to the sea for them to try and catch a boat back home!"

Gran makes us hot chocolates with marshmallows. We sit and listen to Pa's story as the steam rise from our drinks and the marshmallows turn squishy.

"The Japanese men were kept in Cowra in a big camp," Pa continues. "We went past it on our way into town but I never went inside behind the fences."

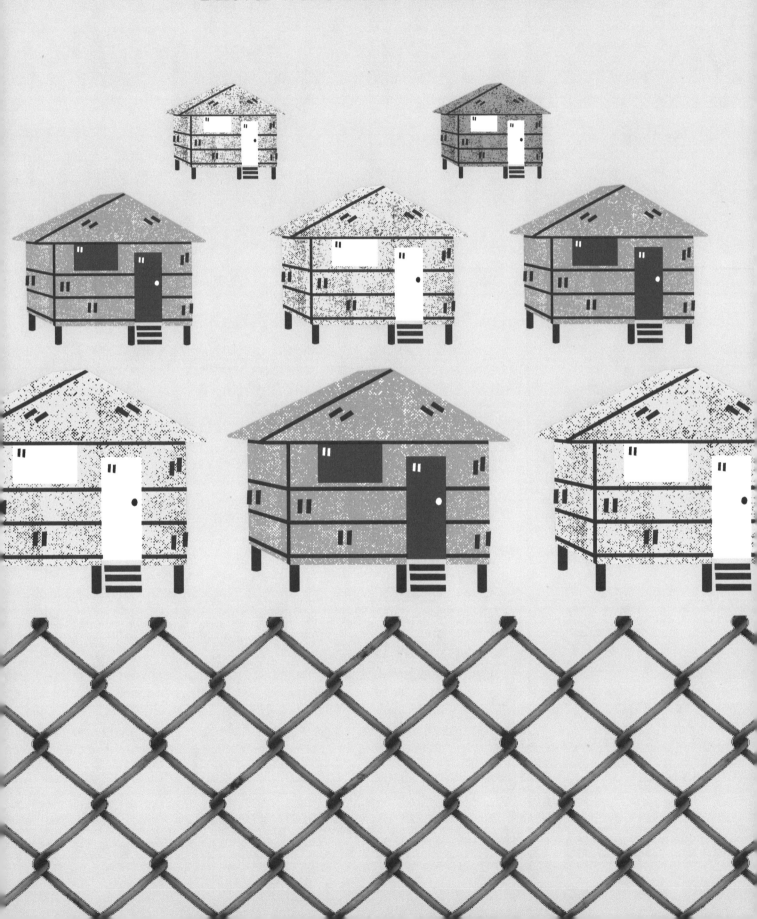

"One night my parents went to a dance in town.
My Dad must have slept in so I got up bright and
early the next morning to do all my chores by myself.
I wanted to go down to the river to go fishing, see,
but I had to collect the eggs first."

"The chook house was open and there inside was the Japanese man hiding with the eggs!"

"Did you scream, Pa?"

"Nup! We didn't say anything! We just stared at each other."

We walk into the loungeroom and my Dad, who has been listening, speaks up and says to Pa, "I've never heard you tell this story before!"

"That's because back then, you weren't supposed to talk about things to do with the war," Pa explains.

"Keep going, Pa! I STILL want to know why he was hiding in the chook house!" I shout.

Pa continues on with his story.
"See, there'd been a big battle down at that
camp I was telling you about. The Japanese
soldiers tried to escape over the fences and some
got away into the hills.

"There were gun shots, huts set on fire and
there was so much chaos that night.

"A lot of men died both Australian and
Japanese but mostly Japanese."

"Why didn't they
just stay prisoners, Pa?"

"Well, I didn't know then, but the Japanese soldiers felt it was shameful to their families and country to be captured. That's why they tried to escape.

"Some were even willing to die."

"Gee, that's a sad story, Pa."

"Well, the story doesn't end there, little mate."

Pa leans forward and touches my hand.
His skin is rough like leather boots but his voice feels warm like
when I sit outside in the spring-time sun.

"Cowra was never the same after that night but some good
things happened too."

"Like what, Pa?"

"People from Cowra buried the Japanese and Australian men side by side. They cared for their graves.
And Japan heard about this.
They were very grateful to know that the men who had died were laid to rest in Australia with dignity and care.

"Ever since, Japanese and Australians stand together at the camp on the anniversary of The Breakout. They remember those who fought and died here in Cowra.

"There are Japanese cherry trees planted in the town and there's even a special Japanese Garden too."

"Two countries that were once at war with each other ended up becoming friends because of the kindness that happened in Cowra.

"I go every year to The Breakout grounds and lay a wreath of flowers for those who lost their lives."
Pa wipes a tear from his eye.

"It's one way I can pay my respects and remember that time in history."

"Can you take me there please, Pa?"

"You bet I can," says Pa, and off we go.

I stand there thinking about the people who had lived in the camp and the ones who had died there too. "Wow, Pa! I'm glad there's no war here now.

"Thank you for telling me this story. I'm going to tell my class about it on Monday at school."

"I can't wait to come back for another visit to Cowra."

About the Author

Lusi Austin is a lover of stories. She and her husband, Brett, and their five children live in the Central West of NSW. As a homeschooling Mum, Lusi was interested in passing on an understanding of the local history to her children. She wanted the information to be accessible to all children and felt the best way to achieve this would be to create Jack's fictitious story based on the real events of The Cowra Breakout.

To learn more about The Cowra Breakout, please visit
https://cowravoices.wordpress.com/ or
https://visitcowra.com.au/ or
The Cowra Breakout Association on Facebook:
https://www.facebook.com/CowraBreakoutAssociation/

Connect with Lusi at www.thathomeschoollife.com.au

CPSIA information can be obtained
at www.ICGtesting.com
Printed in the USA
LVHW072102101121
702988LV00007B/196